BUSHBABY

Copyright © 1991 by Adrienne Kennaway

The moral right of the author/illustrator has been
asserted

This edition published 1998 by Happy Cat Books, Bradfield,
Essex CO11 2UT

A CIP catalogue record for this book is available from the
British Library

ISBN 1 899248 57 9 Paperback
ISBN 1 899248 62 5 Hardback

Printed in Singapore by Imago

BUSHBABY
ADRIENNE KENNAWAY

Happy Cat Books

Bushbaby was always hungry. His favourite food was figs – big, juicy, mouth-watering figs. "Can I go and look for some figs?" he asked his mother one day.

"If you like," she said. "But don't go too far."

Bushbaby lived in a forest by the sea. He jumped from tree to tree, looking for figs. But all the figs he found were little and hard and bitter. They weren't good to eat at all. Where, oh where, could he find some ripe, luscious ones?

"Please, have you seen any juicy figs?" he asked the
colobus monkeys, who lived in the banana grove.

"No figs," said the monkeys. "Come and play with us,
Bushbaby."

"No, thank you," said Bushbaby. "I'm too hungry to play
games."

Bushbaby went to find shy Gennet, who lived in a hollow tree.

"Please, have you seen any juicy figs?" he asked.

Gennet shook her head. "Why don't you ask Heron? He is old and wise. He will tell you where to find some juicy figs."

Heron lived in the mangroves.

"Please, have you seen any juicy figs?" asked Bushbaby.

Heron nodded. "If you follow that path to the island you will find the juiciest figs in the world. But beware! Monitor guards the tree and he is very fierce."

As Bushbaby bounded away Heron called after him, "And watch the tide. Soon the path will be under the water. So hurry, hurry!"

As Bushbaby hopped and bounded across the sandy path, crabs dived for cover in the coral pools.

At last he came to the island. Now, where was the tree Heron had told him about, the tree with the juiciest figs in the world?

There was the tree! Tall and strong, with spreading branches full of ripe fruit. Just looking at it made Bushbaby's mouth water. He couldn't wait to eat all those delicious figs. He would eat and eat until he was full!

Bushbaby took a flying leap into the tree. But he hadn't seen Monitor, the giant lizard, asleep in the stripy shadows.

Mmmm! That was the sweetest fig he had ever tasted.
He ate another ... and another. The juice ran down his
chin and made his fingers sticky.

Bushbaby leaped from branch to branch, greedily eating
every fig he could see. He startled a praying mantis and
almost trod on a centipede.

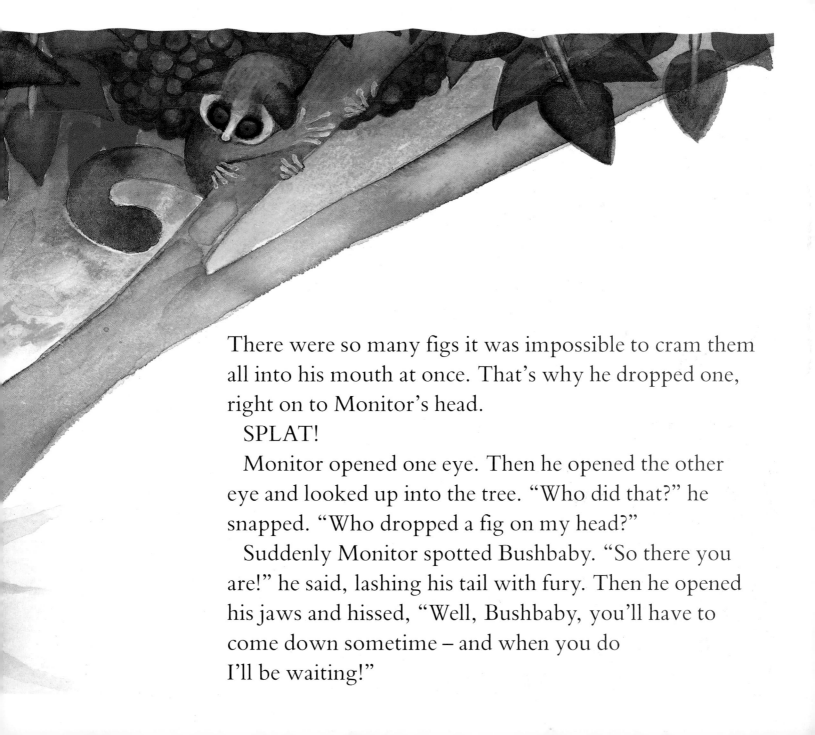

There were so many figs it was impossible to cram them all into his mouth at once. That's why he dropped one, right on to Monitor's head.

SPLAT!

Monitor opened one eye. Then he opened the other eye and looked up into the tree. "Who did that?" he snapped. "Who dropped a fig on my head?"

Suddenly Monitor spotted Bushbaby. "So there you are!" he said, lashing his tail with fury. Then he opened his jaws and hissed, "Well, Bushbaby, you'll have to come down sometime – and when you do I'll be waiting!"

Bushbaby was so frightened that he climbed the tree –
higher and higher, up and up, until he reached the top.

Soon it began to grow dark. The evening sky was full
of flying foxes, gliding and swooping over his head. And
now the sandy path was covered by water. He would
have to stay in the tree all night! His mother would be
dreadfully worried about him.

But the worst thing was that he had the most terrible
pain in his stomach. He wished now he hadn't eaten
so many figs.

At last the stars grew pale and the new day came. But Monitor still waited at the foot of the tree, hissing and spitting. "I must jump for the beach," thought Bushbaby. "But it is so far away."

"Jump, Bushbaby!" hissed Monitor. "Jump and I'll catch you in my waiting jaws." And Bushbaby was so frightened that he sprang from the tree – up and up, higher and higher, his tail flying out behind him. It was the biggest jump he had ever made.

Bushbaby landed safely on the beach. He scampered back
along the sandy path while Monitor lashed his tail on the
shore. But he couldn't catch Bushbaby now.

His mother was overjoyed to see him. He told her all
about his adventures – and about his terrible stomach-ache.

"I'm not surprised, after eating all those figs, you
greedy thing," said his mother. "Your trouble is that
your eyes are bigger than your stomach!"